Annie's PLAID SHIRT

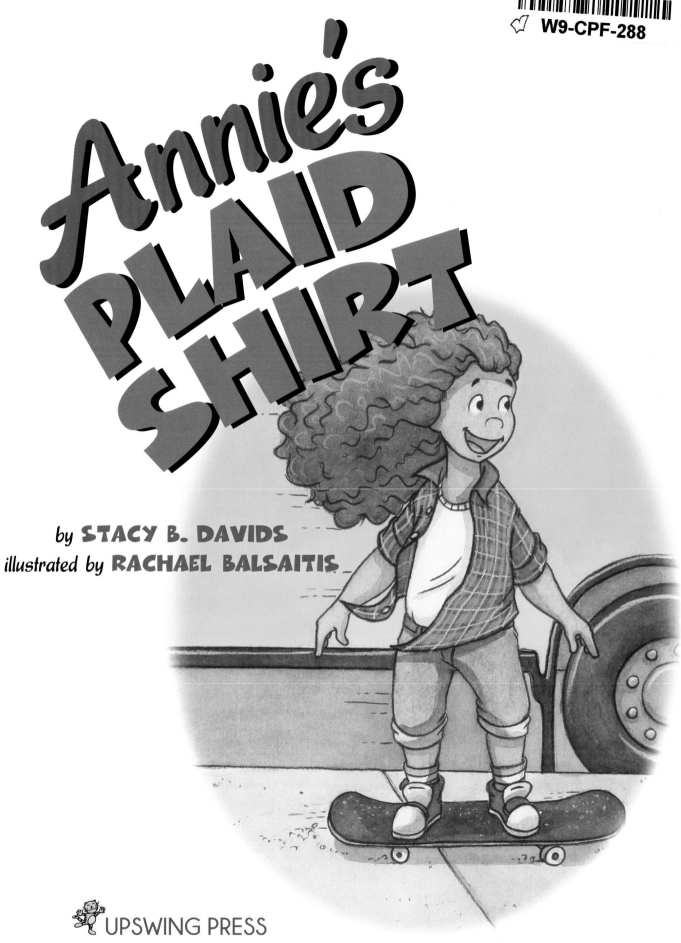

by STACY B. DAVIDS

illustrated by RACHAEL BALSAITIS

UPSWING PRESS

Florida * USA

 UPSWING PRESS

1690 NE 191st Street, Suite 308
North Miami Beach, FL 33179

info@upswingpress.com
www.upswingpress.com

Printed and bound in the United States of America
First Edition
10 9 8 7 6 5 4 3
LCCN 2015949145
ISBN 978-0-692-51245-6

book bridge press

This book was expertly produced by Book Bridge Press
www.bookbridgepress.com

For my mom, Norma, my husband, Rick,
my SCBWI critique group,
and everyone who stays true to themselves
in the face of adversity.
—S. B. D.

For Sara and your many plaid shirts,
and for all those who wear what makes them happy.
—R. B.

Annie loved her plaid shirt.

She went to school in her plaid shirt.

She went to parties in her plaid shirt.

She painted in her plaid shirt.

Annie did *everything* in her plaid shirt.

But one day Annie's mom said, "Let's go to the mall. Tomorrow is Uncle Benny's wedding. Your brother needs a new suit, and you need a nice dress."

"I'll be wearing my plaid shirt," said Annie.

"Oh no," Mom said. "It looks like an old tablecloth. You must wear a dress to the wedding."

"Absolutely not," said Annie. "I'm wearing my plaid shirt."

"We'll see," said Mom.

At the mall, Mom bought Albert a new suit. "Annie," she said, "will you at least try on some dresses for me? Maybe you'll find one you like."

"Yicchh!" replied Annie.

"Please, just this one time?"

"O-o-okay, fine," Annie pouted. "If I have to."

Annie tried on lots of dresses.

But they all felt wrong.

"Please," Mom begged. "Just one more?"

Annie saw the hopeful look on her mom's face.
She agreed to try on just one more.

"It's perfect!" said Mom. "You look so beautiful!"

When they arrived home, Annie ran to her room and slammed the door.

She wished her mom understood her.
Annie felt weird in dresses. She was happiest
when she wore her plaid shirt.
Why couldn't her mom see that?

"Why can't Annie wear what she wants to wear?"
asked Albert.

"I want Annie to be herself. But I'm worried about
what other people will think," Mom said.
"Little girls always wear dresses to weddings."

The next morning, they all rushed to get ready for the wedding. Annie frowned at the dress.

Then she had an idea.

Mom wondered what was taking the kids so long. She started to worry. *I should have let Annie wear her plaid shirt,* she thought.

But it was too late.

"Come on, kids!" she called. "We have to leave now."

Annie and Albert giggled and yelled, "Be right there!"

"Well," said Annie. "What do you think?"

"It's perfect!" said Mom. "You look so beautiful!"

"Of course," said Annie. "I'm wearing my plaid shirt."

STACY B. DAVIDS, PhD, is a licensed clinical psychologist and currently works as a school psychologist. She's also a former special education teacher. Her inspiration for writing *Annie's Plaid Shirt* came from feeling pressure throughout her life to conform to society's rules about gender. Even as a baby she reportedly yanked pink bows out of her hair. As an adult she says, does, and wears what she wants.

Stacy lives in Miami, Florida. Just a few of her favorite things are cats, chocolate, and of course, plaid shirts. Learn more at www.stacybdavids.com.

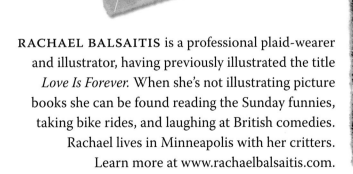

RACHAEL BALSAITIS is a professional plaid-wearer and illustrator, having previously illustrated the title *Love Is Forever.* When she's not illustrating picture books she can be found reading the Sunday funnies, taking bike rides, and laughing at British comedies. Rachael lives in Minneapolis with her critters. Learn more at www.rachaelbalsaitis.com.